230

baby animal tales

Goodnight, Little Sea Otter

This book belongs to:

MAGIC CAT PUBLISHING

NEW YORK

Once upon an ocean, there was a little sea otter.
She lived above a great underwater
forest of seaweed.

Little Sea Otter grew and grew until she was
big enough to start her lessons.

"Today, we are going to learn how to swim down to the
very bottom of the sea forest like the big otters,"
said her mommy.

Little Sea Otter was afraid
of the cold and dark.

But her mommy gave her a big hug,
which made her feel braver.

Down Little Sea Otter went,
deeper and deeper, paddling
with her paws into the depths of
the seaweed forest.

She couldn't see in the deep, dark water, but she could hear her mommy whistling, so she swam after her.

Her mommy guided her back to
the surface of the ocean.

"What a brave little sea otter!" said her mommy,
and she gave Little Sea Otter a big hug.

"Now, let's find some food to eat," said her mommy.
Little Sea Otter tried to catch a crab on the rocks . . .

. . . but it pinched her paw
with its big claw.

"OW!"

Then, she tried to pick up
a sea urchin, but it pricked
her with its sharp spines.

"OW, OW, OW!" she cried.
"My paw hurts!"

A big hug from her mommy soon
made Little Sea Otter feel better.

Then, her mommy showed her how to
open a clam using a stone.

Bish, bash, bosh!

Little Sea Otter tried very hard,
but the clam refused to budge.
It made her feel sad.

"Learning takes time, Little Sea Otter," said her mommy, and she comforted her with a big hug. "Let's try again tomorrow."

They settled down to sleep.

"Squeak, squeak, squeak!"

A noise woke up Little Sea Otter.

She looked around and saw a baby sea otter that was even smaller than her.

"I'm cold and hungry and
I want my mommy," said the baby.

Little Sea Otter knew just what to do.

First, she opened a clam for the baby to eat.

Bish, bash, bosh!

Then, Little Sea Otter
gave the baby a big hug to help her be
brave until, at last, her mommy came back.

"Hugs can help make everything better, can't they?"
said Little Sea Otter to her own mommy later with a yawn.

"And that," said her mommy,
"is the most important lesson of all."

Goodnight, Little Sea Otter!

The illustrations in this book were created digitally.
Set in Above the Sky, Recoleta, and Cabin.

Library of Congress Control Number 2021949384
ISBN 978-1-4197-6021-1

Printed and bound in China
10 9 8 7 6 5 4 3 2 1

Abrams Books are available at special discounts when purchased in quantity for premiums and promotions
as well as fundraising or educational use. Special editions can also be created to specification. For details, contact
specialsales@abramsbooks.com or the address below.

ABRAMS The Art of Books
195 Broadway, New York, NY 10007
abramsbooks.com